STILL NIGHT IN L.A.

A DETECTIVE NOVEL

ARAM SAROYAN

THREE ROOMS PRESS

NEW YORK

Special thanks to Peter and Kat for their humor and bravery.

Still Night in L.A.
A detective novel by Aram Saroyan

ISBN: 978-1-941110-33-1 (Trade Paper)
ISBN: 978-1-941110-34-8 (ebook)
Library of Congress Control Number: 2015935229

COVER PHOTOGRAPH:
Copyright © Armenak Saroyan

INTERIOR PHOTOGRAPHS:
Copyright © Aram Saroyan

COVER AND INTERIOR DESIGN:
KG Design International
katgeorges.com

PUBLISHED BY
Three Rooms Press
New York, NY
threeroomspress.com

DISTRIBUTED BY
Publishers Group West
pgw.com

To
John Densmore
and
Michael C. Ford

It was one of those blue and lavender nights when the luminous color seems to have been blown over the scene with an air brush. Even the darkest shadows held some purple.

NATHANAEL WEST
The Day of the Locust

STILL NIGHT IN L.A.

1

SHE WAS TALL AND STRIKING WITH a face that betrayed her youth more than she probably realized. She let me into a one-bedroom top-floor apartment at the Gaylord on Wilshire west of Vermont. It was a windy but sunny November day, and the vista on old Hollywood from the northern exposure went all the way to the HOLLYWOOD sign.

"Look, this is kind of weird, I guess . . ." She hesitated. "I've been worried."

We were both standing on the wood floor in the living room, which had only a little furniture.

"Okay to sit down?" I asked, hoping that she would sit down too.

"Oh my God!" she said. "I'm sorry. Please." She indicated a chair with straw matting beside a little writing desk.

"How about you?" I said. There was another chair and a sofa against the wall with a white bed sheet tucked in as a slipcover.

"I'm going to stand for a minute, if that's okay. I feel better on my feet right now."

She was the type of woman who would make men's eyes light up when she walked into a restaurant, but she wasn't my type, for which I felt lucky. It's so much easier not to be attracted to your client. God has given thieves perfect eyebrows and liars alabaster arms and it's distracting and dangerous.

"Can I get you some coffee?"

"No, thanks," I said, taking the seat. "What can I do for you?"

"That's the trouble," she said, "I'm not sure. I think somebody might be trying to kill me. Oh, my God, I can't believe I said that!" She turned to me and let go with a five-alarm smile. It was blinding and incongruous. I recovered. I wasn't sure what was going on, but a lot of the time that comes with the territory. The trick is not to make up your mind too quickly and hope you won't be physically hurt during the interim.

"Well," I said, standing up more or less involun-tarily, as if a seated position might make me more vulnerable, as in my experience it had. I had been hit from behind a number of times, blindsided, somebody bringing something hard down on my head. "I always find in this sort of situation it helps if I can get a little history, you know, where you came from and what your family was like, all the way to here."

"No problem. Listen," she said, "do you like lasagna, because I've got some leftovers from Spago that I can heat up in a second."

I told her I was fine, and pulled out my note-book and wrote "Anita Holbrook" at the top of a new page.

I drove up to Sunset when I left her apartment. The summer was over. There was a little wind. You read the seasons in L.A. by such nuances. I made it a handholding job, with maybe the possibility of more than handholding, if one wanted it, and felt a little guilty about taking my weekly per diem and expenses. I stopped at a branch of my bank and made the deposit. I decided to look in on things at the Gaylord later that day without bothering my client.

2

THE MURDER SCENE WASN'T A BLOODY one, and less garish than many others, but I kept flashing back to the very young woman Anita Holbrook had been, between the lines and the Hollywood sheen. Returning to the Gaylord, I'd discovered a police blockade. Detective Axelson with the East Hollywood Division was the man in charge of the crime scene, and we had skated around each other most recently half a year before at a jewel robbery that turned out to be insurance fraud. I'd been hired by the perpetrator as a distraction and Axelson had assembled the case while I was still on salary with the criminal.

"Yo, Dick Tracy," he greeted me. "Who invited you?"

"Nobody—now," I said. The apartment had been turned into a crime scene—tape on the floor, a forensic tech with a notepad and a photographer with a strobe flash. Out the bedroom window the light was hitting the sides of the buildings differently than it had that morning.

As a young cop, I took criminals personally, which is a bad mistake. To be outraged by a politician or a businessman might make sense in the normal course of events, where you have a voting booth or the Better Business Bureau as more or less immediate forms of redress. But to be offended by an extortionist, a kidnapper, or a murderer is like arguing with air pollution.

"When did you see her?" Axelson said, turning back to me at the outer edge of the big front room. Her mostly naked body was visible on the made bed in the bedroom and showed signs of post-mortem lividity.

"Around eleven this morning." It was just after three. "I can tell you I'm on this for another week, unless someone wants her money back. I need to see the body."

"And?" Axelson said, wanting any information I had.

"Yeah, we'll talk," I said.

"This job is weird, like a semi-pro kind of feel to it."

SHE WAS A BEAUTIFUL YOUNG WOMAN, and, as you saw in some deaths, her face was in a repose so deep it seemed to echo an ancestral earth. There was, I knew, an Italian mother and a Danish father.

"I don't see any signs of a struggle," Axelson said behind me.

"Maybe she left them on the perpetrator."

"We figure the swabs we've done are going to come up positive for intercourse."

"This must have happened only a little while after I saw her."

"What're you doing right now? Have you eaten?"

"Yeah, sure . . ."

"I know a place. Mexican. Just a few doors down from the West Side Pavilion."

"WE GOT A LAWYER ON HER answering machine," Axelson told me at a two seater at La Serenata on Pico. I had an iced tea while he lit into the shrimp cocktail.

"Are you going to share that?"

"Maybe, after I hear what you've got."

I told him what I had. She was twenty-six years old; she'd been working an AA program for the past three years; had started making good money modeling; and was dating a lawyer she wanted to keep to one side of my investigation because it could mess up a budding romance. She'd spent a couple of years living with a performance artist named Skeet, who was, she'd told me, about my age.

3

IN THE EARLY MORNING I WALKED down to the Third Street Promenade Mall from my apartment in Santa Monica. I could see the little designs the sun worked through the grass and trees and on buildings in the relative quiet of this time—the few others on California Street at that hour going about their business. In the early morning, one idea—like a cup of coffee—is enough to sustain movement.

My cell vibrated as I carried an espresso to one of three free tables at the coffee kiosk opposite Hennessey & Ingalls on the Third Street Mall.

The text was from my office, a studio on Colorado and Seventh Street. I sat down at the table and decided to hold off for a moment. I needed the caffeine. The drink was raw and full of grounds but it did the trick. I called Amy, my secretary—as I sometimes liked to think of her— at the office.

"A lawyer phoned. He lives at the Gaylord."

"That's where the girl was."

"I'm sorry, but you should always tell me these things. It's very young Hollywood," Amy said. "I had that date with Keanu's stand-in, remember, last November, and he took me to the bar there, the Bounty."

"Thank God I know you."

Amy laughed her gorgeous laugh. She was in her thirties, working an AA program for the last five years, recovering from a bankruptcy. If she ran out of cash, she had to sell something, or borrow from a string of loser boyfriends. She was the most ebullient person I knew.

"You stop that," she said. "You *pay* me, remember? Why else would I talk to you when you don't know what's cool?"

"I better call him."

"Yeah, I almost gave him your number, but I remembered what you said about your state of mind, sir."

4

At two that afternoon, the Bounty, the bar in the lobby of the Gaylord, was almost empty. Still, a young movie star entered and exited a couple of times in the ten minutes I stood there waiting for David Newton to identify himself. This movie star had been making several million dollars a picture since he was about seventeen, and it was because he projected something plain-spoken and

decent in a world of extraterrestrial projectiles
and whatnot. Now he was maybe twenty-three
and at least momentarily at loose ends. The bartender, who looked like Charlie Sheen without
the irony, was a friend of his. There was mention
of a Debra and mention of a Forrest. None of it
made any sense to me but it was pleasant to be at
some sort of hub, some sort of molecular center
of gravity. The movie star was like an important
particle looking for a landing. Maybe it wasn't
clear thinking, but early afternoon deep in Los
Angeles isn't made for clarity. Up on Hollywood
Boulevard people were endeavoring to sell pieces
of soul and self like damaged soup cans at dis-
count. I put down the glass of Amstel Light after
another sip.

"Excuse me, are you Michael Shepard?"

I turned around and looked into a plump even-
featured face.

"You must be Mr. Newton."

He smiled. "Shall we sit down in one of these
booths?"

"Sure."

I took the glass of beer and the bottle and
walked to a corner booth. He signaled the

bartender and in another moment a vodka on the rocks was delivered.

"Thanks for coming," he said after a quick sip.

"Well," I said, "I appreciated your calling me first."

"Meaning what?" Newton said, giving me a sharp look.

"Just that—as I'm sure you know—you're on her answering machine."

"I knew it!" he said. "So, then, I guess she didn't get that message."

"Maybe not." I looked at him without trying to make too much of it.

"Did you have something you wanted to tell me?"

"No," he said a decibel louder. "I mean yes, sure," he said in a softer tone. "We were seeing each other. It wasn't that serious yet, but this is hitting me kind of hard."

I explained that I had been hired by Anita Holbrook for a week and also let him know that he would most likely be hearing from Detective Axelson.

5

I woke up because the phone had rung and it rang again.

"Hey, it's time for us to do a power breakfast." It was Axelson. "You're starting to step on my lines."

"How?" I said. It was six thirty-two in the morning.

"You go to the Bounty and talk to David Newton and even tell him I'm running the investigation.

The guy's got his *lawyer* phoning me, telling me his client won't talk to me."

"Why?"

"You tell me. Do you like the Bagel Nosh at Seventeenth and Wilshire?"

"Sure, when?"

"I'm here."

I got dressed, picked up the *Times* on the doorstep, and put it on the front table. Wilshire Boulevard was semi-deserted and coolish in the dawn light. Axelson was married, I knew, though I'd never met his wife, and he had to be close to retirement. He had a mobile home in Newport Beach I'd once rented for a week with Stephen and Vera.

I GOT IN THE SERVICE LINE at the Bagel Nosh and ordered the bacon and eggs special. They gave me the plastic number to put at the table. I got coffee, and found Axelson at a corner window table.

"David Newton is a lawyer himself," I said sitting down.

"Exactly the point," Axelson said, holding out his coffee cup for a refill from a waitress. He didn't have a plastic number.

"You going to eat?" I asked.

"No, no. You go ahead. I can't take this kind of food."

"Then why are we here?" I said. "Neither can I."

"It reminds me of the old days," Axelson said. "Here's your poison."

The waitress put down the plate and went away.

"Eat it," Axelson said, looking at the food. "It won't kill you."

I bit into a piece of crisp bacon. "I mean Newton's a lawyer himself."

Axelson told me that the people at the Gaylord were into a recreational heroin thing that had gotten ugly a couple of weeks back when a twenty-three-year-old actress had leaped or been pushed to her death from her studio apartment there. The autopsy indicated heroin, probably an overdose. He suspected that David Newton was shoring himself up against possible exposure in that case, or a possible bust for heroin. There was nothing to put him at the Anita Holbrook crime scene.

"We're looking at this as a possible multiple, and I need you to check out some leads to keep things off balance."

"You've got a suspect?"

"The weirdo poet or performance artist or whatever. Swings both ways."

"Skeet."

"We've talked to him before and I looked over some reports. Talk about a chip on his shoulder. This guy single-handedly birthed the twenty-first century and hasn't received the recognition he's due."

"How'd you get him into the picture? She talked about him."

He nodded again. "Anyway, I've been thinking."

"I'm sure you have," I said. The LAPD wasn't paying me.

"You're a good listener. You're exactly the type of guy this guy would like."

"Jesus. What're you saying?"

"Go to his variety show Saturday at Banshee's on Fairfax. It'll be a hoot."

6

THAT EVENING STEPHEN AND I MET up for the first time in a while. Cirque du Soleil is a kind of Chaplin-esque off-kilter ballet with people running here and there with great purpose for no reason, and rising from beneath manhole covers with bemused aspects. The whole thing subverts your expectations about what a circus is, and then delights you with itself.

Stephen laughed a couple of times during the performance and then there was an intermission. We stood outside in the pleasant night air beside the Santa Monica pier, where the Circus pitched its tent each year.

"That was cool," he said. He was taller than me now, dressed in a T-shirt, baseball cap, and baggy jeans.

A movie star, a pale delicate blond wearing a black sweater over jeans and little makeup, went by with a man friend and someone who could have been her mother.

"So how are you?" I said. "How's the job?" He was a security guard at a mall in Simi Valley. He was enrolled in two courses at Moorpark Junior College but had had ongoing trouble with substance abuse.

Stephen asked if I'd recognized the movie star and I said I had but couldn't remember her name.

"Me neither," he said.

I'd learned at Al-Anon meetings to keep from trying to convince him of things and just get out of the way of his own Higher Power, or call it the reality principle.

"What've you been up to?"

"Nothing much," he said. "I may go snow-boarding with Alex."

"You're really getting into it."

"I can't believe how much fun it is. I never had so much fun in my life. And I keep thinking, you know, if I get good enough I can teach it."

"You mean you'd move up to Big Bear."

"Or Boulder."

"Have you talked to your mother about it?"

"Not yet, but I don't necessarily need your permission, you know," he said, smiling in his puckish mode. "I mean I'm twenty-one now."

"What about college?"

"I'm taking two courses."

Stephen seemed about as ready for college as Justin Bieber but these days people in their late twenties, thirties, and even forties went back to school.

7

AMY WAS GOING TO TAKE THE afternoon off to be with her "little sister," Tracy, a fifteen-year-old black girl who lived in South Central with an aunt and her husband. The girl was running with the wrong crowd, which might have been the *only* crowd where she lived. Her boyfriend was probably a gang member, Amy thought. She wanted Tracy to finish high school and maybe go to college.

"In other words," she said, "I want her to have everything I don't have, and probably never will." She laughed.

I smiled from my desk diagonally across the room.

"I don't know how we're supposed to guide young people . . ." I said.

"You're speaking about me, right? The young person . . ." She laughed again.

Amy wasn't bad looking, in the way of a thirty-something jazz singer. Wanting to keep a good—and only—employee, I'd long ago opted to keep a proprietary distance.

"How's your son?" she said out of the blue.

"He's happier than I was at his age."

"Is that good?"

"He's over twenty-one. I guess he has an opinion. The only one that matters."

"I see you've been working your program," she said. The phone rang and she picked it up.

I'd come to the office to get ready for another meeting with Efren de Guzman, the director of the Torrance Learning Center, who had hired me for six months on retainer to look into funding improprieties in the local arm of the federal job training program in Torrance.

8

THE SCENE SATURDAY NIGHT AT BANSHEE'S, just south of Venice Boulevard on Lincoln was a big L.A. grab bag with the usual neo-vaudevillians. A girl named Ann Lane got up and read a poem that I couldn't really follow, but there was something self-contained and yet vulnerable about her: she let you see she was a person. There was prolonged applause at the end. She smiled in a self-conscious, charming way and walked over to the bar where I was standing and ordered a glass of Perrier.

"On the house," the bartender said.

"That was wonderful," I said.

"Thank you," she said.

"Do you happen to know if Skeet's here tonight?"

"He should be, and, knowing Skeet, he *will* be."

"Loves publicity or something?" I said.

"That's the general idea, yes."

"A bit of a wild man, I take it."

"You sound like a cop or something."

She looked directly at me and didn't smile.

"I'm a private investigator," I said. "A young woman was murdered on Tuesday right after she hired me to find out if someone was going to kill her. She had Skeet's name in her address book."

"I'm sorry. I think I heard about it. But that's not unusual about Skeet, although I personally don't know why."

"What's not unusual?"

"Oh, I just meant about his name in her address book. Gosh, not the murder."

Skeet, a solidly built older guy got to the microphone about twenty minutes later.

"Alright," he said. "When I was walking the streets looking for one person who believed that a lower-class yid-mick from Philly could have any potential as a writer, there were one or two people who encouraged me, and the most important of these was a Puerto Rican woman, an early riot girl you might say, who liked to read novels by Jack Kerouac and Raymond Chandler . . ."

After he came off the stage, he worked his way through the crowd, stopping here and there for kisses and/or conversation. He eyed me with a half-smile and then ordered some water with a twist of lemon.

"Hey, sweetheart, how are you?" he said to Ann Lane.

"I'm fine, Skeet. Enjoyed your show."

"Well, thanks. I enjoyed yours. Even noticed a couple of things, well, I may mistakenly believe you learned from me." He smiled.

"Could be," Ann Lane said, "but I promise to thank you on the album, okay?"

"That's all I ever ask of any of the people I help— just that they not forget who helped out. Album?"

9

LATE NIGHT OR MORE ACCURATELY EARLY morning television is bad for the soul, but some nights I find it hard to sleep even after all my senses have crashed. The hard drive is down, but I'm still awake. I found myself watching an infomercial about a designer brain. It was done with electronic waves, no pills, like some kind of low wattage electro-shock treatment. There was an 800 number.

There was a level of desperation to this fakery . . . or for all I know it actually worked. There was an actor who had experienced a quickening of his career after a few jolts. There was a secretary who had discovered that the only reason things hadn't been going better at her job was that she never smiled.

"A DESIGNER BRAIN," ANN LANE SAID on the phone the next day. "You sound like you need a meeting."

"Which one?" I asked. "And how do I know Skeet won't be there?"

"Just avoid AA. He sponsors half of the West Side. Guys who have development deals and drive Porsches meet him for coffee at Joe's Diner after their Pilates sessions for $150 an hour."

"Pilates?"

"It's very expensive exercise?"

"With food, or what?"

"No food. It's about a balance."

"I know a pretty good Mexican place on Pico."

"You want me to talk about Skeet."

"Not really, but I guess I should ask."

"And I see the way you look at me. You're way too old for me."

"I'm a detective."

"A likely story."

10

"I GOT SOME TECH WORK THAT should be done in a day or two," Axelson told me over the phone. "So I want you to stay on him, but I don't want him to know you. Can you handle it?"

"Surveillance? It's my business."

"Look," he said, "can you go with me for a day or two on this? I'm short-staffed here. This girl isn't priority one, but we're thinking there's another one, about three years ago."

"This is the multiple angle?"

"Right . . ."

"Who was the victim?"

"Val Raven."

"Oh . . ."

Hollywood High, April Rain, and others had been special movies for a lot of people. Then one day he didn't show up on the set of a new movie and was never seen again.

"They were lovers. Skeet was in B pictures for a while, was in some noir picture, probably through Raven. Anyway, we could never prove it, but he was a prime suspect. I need a favor. And, by the way, this'll wipe our slate clean."

SKEET HAD A COTTAGE ON POINT View in the Fairfax area, which was a poor situation for surveillance: a tree-lined street with zero activity. It was a mild and sunny afternoon. The street was empty and quiet except for a faint roar off Pico boulevard to the south. Skeet had been in his house for going on twelve hours and I needed a break—a shower, some actual sleep, something other than the stale roast from Starbucks I'd had in a thermos for about a week and a couple of banana-and-jelly sandwiches. If I ate anything, it seemed like a nap tried to take over.

Trying to stay alert, I was also listening to Helen Borgers on KJAZ, out of Long Beach and she played something by Charles Mingus that was as melodic as an Ellington standard. I remembered Mingus standing in Bermudas looking like a Teamster at the old hungry i in San Francisco and tangling with some bruiser in the front row who had heard that the big man was sensitive.

Then Skeet backed out in his blue Mustang and headed down toward Pico.

11

I saw him take a left onto La Cienega from about two blocks back and figured he was headed for the 10 Freeway, the 10 East or the 10 West. I could have used Axelson's backup just then, or a helicopter adjunct. After my early days with the Marin County PD equipment, I never had a reason to use a car phone before they came into currency but then they immediately grew indispensable. Up until the invention of the personal computer I never had an impulse to "move a paragraph" to a different part of a report, either, but the same thing happened.

By the time I made it to La Cienega he was nowhere in sight and traffic was slow. I had just about given up when I saw a flash of blue turning onto the 10 West. I prayed he wasn't going to take the next several off-ramps before I could find him again.

I caught up to him around Cloverfield and then began hanging back.

He took the Lincoln exit and headed south and then surprised me by pulling abruptly into the single metered parking spot in front of Books, a used bookstore where I sometimes browsed.

I parked about a block further down after I saw him go through the open door.

A couple of old geezers run the shop, one of whom doesn't seem to have both oars in the water. "In a surprise a few months ago they hired a young woman named Samantha who has read everything by acclaimed writers of the day like Pynchon and DeLillo and also happens to be beautiful.

When I walked in the door, I saw that Skeet was at the register. I didn't want to engage Samantha so I moved to the closest hardcover shelves to keep out of sight. The place is full to bursting with books, very poorly organized, and, especially in the hardcover shelves, very poorly lit.

"You have an opportunity, that's all," I heard Skeet say in a softer tone than I'd heard at Banshee's.

"I have a job," Samantha said.

"I told you how to handle that," Skeet said.

I pulled out my cell phone in the dark biography section and texted Axelson. Then I put the cell into vibrate mode and waited, looking at titles in the semi-dark.

12

Axelson called quickly. We both figured he was going to cut and run. They were working to get a warrant for some trace liftings from his apartment to match the crime scene and, if they could keep legal protocol, they figured they had their man.

Skeet left Books while I was on the cell and I followed him out as I finished the call. He was gone by the time I reached the sidewalk, not having looked Samantha's way. It was turning dark. I figured he was headed back to the bungalow and hadn't a clue how I was supposed to gain admittance. Axelson was growing more and more like my commanding officer and I kept reminding myself that I wasn't on the payroll. Then I'd remember that Anita Holbrook had paid me.

SKEET ANSWERED THE DOOR OF 1221-1/2 Point View naked from the waist down so that the head of his dick peeked out from under the lip of his T-shirt. I was taken aback.

"Hi," I said, enthusiastically. "You're Skeet, right?"

"Okay," Skeet said and waited.

I thought it was a good idea to give the moment a little ventilation to see where it went, but he was in no rush.

"Hi," I said again picking up the slack and extending a hand. He looked at it and then shook it perfunctorily. "I'm James Redding . . . I'm doing a documentary about the performance art scene in L.A., and about every single person I've talked to has told me I need to get in touch with you. I'm on my way to the airport; I'm heading back to New York tonight. But I took a chance and looked you up in the phone book . . ."

"I'm not in the phone book," Skeet said.

"Oh, I'm thinking of Ann Lane, maybe. Somebody I guess gave me your address . . ."

"Wait a minute . . . I know you . . . from Banshee's, right?"

I nodded. It's nice to see the short-term memory thing kick in in an over-forty.

"Right," I said. "And I can't tell you how important I think this thing is . . . what you're doing . . . performance art. . . . How important I think *you* are. . . . I mean you're giving poetry back to people again."

Skeet's face and posture shifted slightly. "Who did you say you were again?"

"Jamie Redding," I said.

For a second I thought about trying the revolutionary handshake but reminded myself that discretion is the better part of valor. Skeet stepped back then, and I stepped into the apartment.

13

WE DISCUSSED A COUPLE OF THE other players I'd seen at Banshee's and Ann Lane came up. He had put on a pair of pants. I was sitting at a little table in the kitchen area. The place had an unpleasant odor. There was a big poster of Warhol's four flowers. Skeet was moving back and forth between his main room and the little kitchen alcove.

"I like her work," I said casually.

"Look," Skeet said, coming back into the little kitchen area to turn off some hot water. "We all like it. And I'm not saying she shouldn't be in the film. She'll probably end up a lot bigger than me. She's young and pretty and, like I said, I like the work."

He set down a cup of tea in front of me with a tea bag still in it: Celestial Seasoning's Sleepy Time. Then he sat down. I took a sip. The honey had already been added.

"You know, if you want, I can put together a big anthology show at Banshee's and you can film it live . . ."

"That would be great," I said. "When could you get that together by? See, I've got most of my funding squared away but these people really want to see footage."

"Sure," Skeet said. "That's not a problem. . . . Let's see. . . . It's what—November 8th . . . do you want to do it before Christmas?"

I was looking at the knotty pine top of Skeet's little kitchen table when I noticed that it was doing a kind of shimmy. Then I looked up at Skeet, and, as my eyes shifted from the table to his face, it seemed as if my eyesight was like a deck of cards being shuffled; I saw the table in successive stuttered frames even though I was seeing Skeet's face at the same time.

14

I SEE THAT STEPHEN HAS LOST his lower teeth and I'm upset and saddened. He speaks some reassurance and I worry that his life is closing down on him. I'm even crying.

MY ASSISTANT AMY WAS STANDING BESIDE my bed and gazing into the middle distance looking uncharacteristically solemn when I woke up in a semi-private room at Midway Hospital. When she turned her gaze to me it took a moment for her to realize my eyes were open.

"Oh, you're up," she said.

Suddenly Axelson was beside her.

"There's the boy," he said, looking directly at me and not shifting his eyes. "Can you speak?"

"Probably," I said.

They both grinned.

"I don't even want to tell you what this guy gave you," Axelson started in, but then stopped. "Do you remember what happened?"

"Not too well," I said. I had a strange taut feeling in my mouth that I remembered from long ago. "Acid?"

"Liquid DMT, so you must have gone up like a solo by the king."

"The king?"

"Benny Goodman. . . . Plus stuff designed to shoot you down even faster."

"To kill me?" I said.

Axelson nodded. "We had to pump your stomach pronto."

"Did you get him?"

Axelson shook his head.

"Leave him alone," Amy said and mentioned I'd slept for almost twenty-four hours.

"Wow," I'd never done that before. "I guess I'm still on this," I said.

They both looked puzzled.

"What day is it?" I said.

"It's Tuesday, noon," Axelson said.

"That's around when I saw her, a week ago."

"So?" Axelson said.

"I can't charge her while I've been unconscious," I said.

Amy looked concerned and then turned to Axelson.

"He's not making sense," she said. Then she looked back at me. "Go back to sleep."

15

WHEN I WOKE UP AGAIN, THE steel taste had gone
from my mouth and I felt light. I lay in bed
thinking that life was interesting, in that, unlike
an old-fashioned battery that just ran down, a
human being could be recharged with sleep, food,
vitamins, and the affections of a fellow human.

I remembered Ann Lane. To my left was a
window and it looked like a nice day outside,

blue sky with a couple of white cloud formations sailing along.

On my right was a curtain and I heard some people talking in Spanish.

I wanted to leave, and it seemed to me that I would be able to do that. A phone rang and after a moment I saw that it was on the shelf beside me. I picked up the receiver and said hello.

"Dad?"

"Hey, buddy."

"Are you alright?" Stephen sounded upset.

"Yeah, I'm fine," I said. "I guess I've been doing a lot of sleeping."

"I wanted to come in, but my car is dust."

"Don't come in. I'm going to be out of here soon."

"Really, when?"

"Today, tomorrow . . ."

A pretty dark-haired nurse appeared from the other side of the curtain, looked at me, whispered something I couldn't make out, smiled, and disappeared behind the curtain again. The discussion in Spanish continued.

"Oh . . ." Stephen said.

"Yeah, so how you doing?"

"Who, me?" Stephen said. "Okay, I guess. Same old same old. . . . But I heard you got hurt bad . . ."

"Who told you?"

"Well, Mom, actually. She's really worried about you, too."

"No need to worry. All in a day's work. Sometimes you run into some trouble out there."

"This is like a murder, huh?"

"Remember I told you that Tupac could have gone another route."

Stephen gave his funny deep short laugh. "I don't know . . ."

"How's your Mom doing?"

"Worried, I guess."

"Well, tell her not to worry."

A lot of my money was going into term life insurance in case I got whacked. It was costing me an arm and a leg.

16

Although my intention had been to keep whatever—largely emotional—momentum had built up in my work on the Holbrook case, Amy had a message from Efren de Guzman, the remedial education contractor whom I'd been working for on retainer, and I needed to put Skeet out of mind for several days.

I admired Efren and his ingenuous dedication
this late in the American day. He was, it seemed,
content to use me and my legwork with various
contractors as some sort of scare tactic at the
monthly public meetings the federal Job Training
Partnership Act mandated for its local providers.
Maybe it did some good. I was sitting beside him
that week at the Torrance Hilton monthly
meeting when an idea having to do with Skeet
took hold of me and nearly caused me to rise out
of my chair.

"What is it?" Efren said.

I pulled myself back to the table. Aurelia
Gompers was speaking about her funding needs
at the Torrance Learning Center. She was the
picture of feisty dedication. Efren had told me
she and Arturo de Leon, the local head of the
program, were cheating on their spouses with
each other.

"It's all about sex," I whispered, grasping at a
nearby straw.

Efren looked at me sideways. Then he nodded.

"Of course you are right. Sometimes I forget."

17

I SAID GOODBYE TO EFREN IN the parking lot.

"Must you leave now?" he said, exuding the gravitas of a boss. "I had hoped we could discuss your insights over a meal."

"I'll get back to you in the morning. Unfortunately I have an appointment."

"But why did you say nothing about it before?"

"I just got a text I've been waiting for, Efren. I'll make it up to you."

"See that you do," he said, smiled, and got into his green Nissan.

I took Sepulveda up to the 110 North, and then caught the 10 West to La Cienega. It was around nine thirty when I parked on Point View and texted Axelson. I waited in the Beemer and Axelson called back in about three minutes.

"Jesus, I'm watching reruns of *Seinfeld.* Jerry Stiller has invented a *man-zier,* this garment for an older guy who develops breasts . . ."

"Detective Axelson?"

"Yeah. What's up?"

"I want to know if it's okay to go into Skeet's cottage."

"Well, we got the warrant. Why?"

"I have a hunch. Lemme check it out, okay?"

"The key's in a baggie in the planter by the hose at the entrance. If you're incorrect, cover your tracks. If you're not, I'll be there and we take the credit."

18

AFTER I FOUND THE KEY I had to go back to the
car for my flashlight because the electricity had
been turned off, or someone had thrown the cir-
cuit breaker and I didn't know where to find it.
With the flashlight on, I saw the furniture all in
place. I stood for a moment in the front room
and cut the beam. I waited for another minute or
so to see if my eyes acclimatized to the dark.

There was a moon out and pretty soon I could at least make out the main clumps of furniture. I wanted to track the smell and figured maybe I could do it better without the light.

I stood by the kitchen table where I'd first noticed it. It was there still, some putrid essence. I went beyond the table to the back door and opened it and stood out on the little wood porch for a moment. It wasn't warm but there wasn't any wind. It was stronger there, I thought. Or maybe just inside the door. I clicked on the flashlight again and got down on my knees to look under the porch. There was about a foot clearance with cinder block joists standing where the porch gave onto the back door.

I stood up again and went into the house and walked through the kitchen and into the front room again where the smell wasn't as strong. Then I walked back to the kitchen table and then to the back door where it was stronger again. The floor in the kitchen was linoleum.

I decided to go home and come back with my toolbox in the morning light.

19

I CARRIED MY TOOLBOX INTO THE cottage with me early the next morning. I took a look at the linoleum in the corner kitchen area. There was a thin strip of wood molding holding it down, which I worked off carefully with a chisel. The linoleum was a sheet and wasn't very evenly glued down. Slowly I worked it up from the corner until I saw a cut line in the plywood floor.

In another hour I had the linoleum cleared over the entire oblong that had been cut, about a four-by-five-foot cut, part of which went under the table where I'd sat that night with Skeet and first noticed the smell. Then I worked on getting up the plywood piece with the chisel and the other side of the hammer. There was a large metal box down there, and the smell was intense.

I got down on the dirt in the hole beside the metal box and saw that it had a padlock on it. I took out my little bandsaw and spent about a quarter of an hour sawing until the lock was cut. The top had to be removed while flush with the lower part, and I did that and put the top on the kitchen floor.

There was a big plastic bag in the box and it was full of something mostly black.

The stench was hard to take. I got out of the hole in the floor and went into the front room and called Axelson.

20

AFTER THE MORNING AT SKEET'S, I noticed at the office that I was fading. Amy told me her boyfriend, a documentary filmmaker who was living on the streets of downtown L.A. to make a film on the homeless, didn't want to have any children because he felt it was dishonorable to bring children into such a miserable world. Did I agree? I began to say something—as if talking might throw my brain into gear—but then realized that Amy had been crying as she was talking and I shut up.

The bag turned out to be full of a body, parts of which had been dismembered—probably to make it fit into the box—and some remains of granulated sugar maybe to speed the deterioration process. We waited a couple of days for the dental records, and then the story went national.

It was Val Raven. Axelson was on TV.

Late on the night of the day the story broke, Vera phoned to say that Stephen had been arrested on a DUI and was being held in the East Valley Station in Camarillo. Both of us sporadically and separately had worked an Al Anon program, and we both knew we weren't supposed to save him.

A minute or so after I put down the phone I got a collect call from Stephen in jail.

"Adrienne Welch says if you'll front me the bail money it won't even go to court until I've had time to figure out my case and get an attorney." Adrienne Welch was Stephen's friend

Jimmy's mother, a woman the program would call an "enabler."

"Who's going to pay for that?"

"Well, I mean, you know . . ."

I asked what had happened.

The story involved having drinks at the local Holiday Inn, followed by an altercation with the bouncer at BJ's in the North Ranch Mall, which he wanted to enter or already had entered because there was a dollar-a-drink special. The police were called, and after Stephen was questioned, he was told not to leave the scene, at which point or soon after he got into his car and drove off.

The police gave chase, Stephen stopped his car on Westlake Boulevard just beyond the 101 South exit and ran. He was tackled around Gelson's Market. He resisted arrest and threw up in the police car.

"I must have been very drunk," he said.

I spoke to the female officer on duty at the East County Jail and got a run down on the charges. Then Stephen called me back and asked again if I would bail him out. When I said no, instead of cursing me, which he would normally do, he told me that he loved me. He had done that one other time, I remembered, also when he was very drunk.

21

THE NEXT MORNING (STEPHEN'S COURT DATE was set for the following afternoon) Amy had scheduled an appointment for me at my office, where I try to spend as little time as possible. I don't usually have a lot of work to do there. It's a medium-sized room on the third floor with a large window looking north on Seventh Street. Amy has her desk in the corner to the immediate left of the door, and my desk is diagonally across the room from hers. When I have a visitor she turns on KUSC, the public radio classical music station.

Jake Ryan was a fifty-something lumbering guy who showed up in a faded purple jogging suit carrying a manila envelope. I led him to the chair in front of my desk and went behind the desk and sat down. By the time I'd sat down he was on the other side of the room looking out the window. There was a Mozart symphony on the radio.

"What can I do for you, Mr. Ryan?"

He turned and looked at me distractedly and then his eyes shifted and he smiled, as if to himself. He seemed to force himself to return to the chair, sit in it, and look at me.

"I'm married to an actress," he said. "The other night, I go with her to a staged reading of a play she's doing, the kind of thing they do a lot of these days. You know, the actors hold the scripts and they just read the thing . . ."

"Sure," I said.

"So the play's about . . . I don't know, it's about a couple of people who eventually are going to fuck. It kind of builds that way. It was alright, except I'm getting the sense that my wife, who's younger than I am, and the kid she's reading it with, are getting worked up."

More surveillance.

"I just want to be sure what's going on. I'm not crazy. She makes me happy. I love her, but my mind gets going and it can take over. You're like a sanity enforcer. I'm going to turn it over to you."

"That's probably a good decision," I said.

I got all the details including an eight by ten glossy of Mrs. Ryan he had brought in the manila envelope. She had a rather turbulent dark look that seemed an off choice for casting agents. Her stats on the back gave her height at five foot three.

As I was leading Mr. Ryan to the door, I noticed Amy at her desk in her white shirt with rolled up sleeves and an extra button undone.

"Goodbye," Jake Ryan said, and his eyes wandered over toward Amy and he smiled and nodded.

"I'll be in touch," I said.

22

I SLEPT THAT NIGHT UNTIL MY usual, around four or so, when I woke up in my bedroom with a diffused pain. Stephen was incarcerated. I myself had never been in jail. I knew my father never had been, either. As for my grandfather, a Lithuanian Jew, who knew? But it seemed a terrible thing in the pre-dawn dark. It was as if society had turned inside out in a family member, and the best that I could do was to let things take their course. Perhaps this was the wake-up call he needed.

VERA AND I MET IN THE lobby of Ventura County Superior Court. She was wearing a basic black suit and looked well. We entered Court Room 11 together and discovered that Adrienne Welch, Stephen's friend's mom, was the only other person present. She was a plump middle-aged woman who had obviously spent some time getting dressed and made up. She greeted us politely and we took seats in the front row, too, leaving a space between us. Stephen was on the other side of a glass panel, sitting in the second row of a two-row bleacher with other identically dressed inmates. I looked at him and he returned my look but didn't nod or smile. Gradually other parents and wives and friends entered the room.

Adrienne Welch struck the wrong note with Vera by suggesting that Stephen was just a kid who'd made a mistake. I was sitting between them. Vera looked across at her.

"Are you working a program?" she asked.

"Am I working a program?"

"Yes," Vera said.

"No. I don't drink."

"Well, you have a son who does, and you don't seem to know how to behave with our son."

I turned to Vera to soften the confrontation. She turned away from me, and by extension Adrienne Welch, without saying anything more.

THE JUDGE WENT ALONG AT A rapid clip. Stephen pled guilty, they dropped the resisting arrest charge, and he was fined and sentenced to four days. With good behavior, he'd already done most of that time. He would be released, the court clerk told me, around midnight. We wouldn't be able to see him until his release.

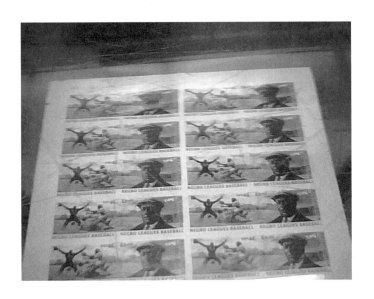

23

I WAS FOLLOWING MRS. JAKE RYAN, whose professional name was Lori Stone. After an audition at Universal, she drove on Lankershim to Highland and down to Third Street, where she parked on the street and wandered in and out of stores. She bought a big art deco lamp at Zipper and squeezed it into her red Accord and fed the meter. Then she went into Aunt Lucy's antique clothing store. It was sunny and cold. I stood across the street at the outdoor newspaper kiosk leafing through *People* and kept thinking about Skeet and Ann Lane and the fact that my son was in the grip of a disease, as opposed to him being right or wrong. If Stephen had cancer I wouldn't try to be his doctor, and I had as little business trying to treat his disease as an addict/alcoholic.

She came out and got into her car. I put the magazine back and jogged to my car and followed her down Third Street. She cut over to Melrose and parked and went into Angeli for lunch. I found parking across the street and thought some more and then stopped thinking and said a prayer. Then I phoned Ann Lane.

"Skeet is nowhere to be found."

"I couldn't believe the story," she said. "I don't know why, but I never believe that sort of thing can happen. How can you be sure it was him?"

"A lot of ways, including DNA. I'd like to talk to you."

"It's really scary."

"Will you be around later today? Everybody's coming up empty and maybe you know something you don't think you know."

"Like what?"

"Anything. Maybe a person. Any lead right now would help."

MRS. RYAN SAID GOODBYE TO A woman friend in front of Angeli and got into her car and drove off, and I followed her down to Vermont, where she took a right and then a left on Wilshire to the Gaylord. She and Mr. Ryan, who was a movie studio CPA, lived in a house in Brentwood. She went into the Bounty a little before three and sat at a table in the almost empty room and I looked the place over again standing at the bar. I had another Amstel Light from Charlie Sheen.

"How're you?" he said, as though he remembered me.

I said I was doing well and asked how he was doing.

"Can't complain," he said. "Would rather be on my board up at Zuma, but if the weather holds, I'll be there Wednesday."

"Surfing," I said and nodded.

"It's good for perspective."

"You mean you can lose it on the job?"

"You mean this place," he said, looking around the establishment. "I've seen a few things that could give you sleepus interruptus," he said and barked a laugh.

I thought it was a little strange for Mrs. Ryan to be here alone. My cell rang. I took it out of my jacket pocket.

24

"I THOUGHT YOU COULD HANDLE THIS without a text," Amy said. "I have a dentist appointment, so I'm leaving early. Remember Laura Fonseca . . . ?"

"Sort of," I said. "I'm occupied here."

"Sorry. Do you want me to go on?"

"Sure, but quickly please."

"She was this young blond discovery of Roger

Norbert's when he made *April Rain*, which was Val Raven's best picture I think."

"Oh, yeah, the girl . . ."

"She was big and then she dropped out of sight . . ."

"Right."

"Anyway, she called. She wants to see you."

"About what?"

"Well, I don't think it's about futures and options," she said laughing.

A thirtyish suit came into the bar. When I put my cell in my pocket and looked over at Mrs. Ryan's table, he was sitting opposite her. After a few minutes they got up and walked out. I looked at Charlie Sheen who was following their departure. When they were gone I put a fifty-dollar bill down on the table by the Amstel Light and asked who the man was. He looked at the fifty and then at me.

"Jesus," he said. "I had you figured for some kind of studio guy."

"How do you know I'm not?"

"Yeah, right," he said. He took the fifty and folded it and put it in his shirt pocket. "Love in the afternoon, I guess. Steve Resta, one of the gang here. Real estate law or something."

"He's at the Gaylord?" I said.

"Yeah," he said.

I put a new fifty down beside the bottle.

"Do you happen to have the room number?"

"These are customers. What's going on?"

"Probably not a helluva lot."

He took up the other fifty, folded it, and put it in his pocket with the other bill. He went to look through a pile of bills by the register.

"612," he said. "I don't know you."

25

ROOM 612 HAD A WESTERN EXPOSURE and it had taken me the rest of the afternoon to arrange to have a telescope with a semi-X-ray capacity for certain window treatments up on a roof on Western. I had access to the roof because of a business eviction case I'd worked for the landlord several years back.

Laura Fonseca was on my mind while I got the scope—from a trade rental service on Westin—assembled. A classic soap ad of a blond, if Marilyn Chambers hadn't forever altered the concept. Perfect complexion and she and Val Raven had once been an item. Somehow or other you cared about Raven, a volatile adolescent in his first film, *Bronx Bingo*, who never seemed to shake that image and grow into adulthood. He had a wounded, sexually ambiguous persona and the liaison with Fonseca may have been studio hype.

I had the scope aimed several blocks east. Along with its western exposure, room 612 had the straight white vertical blinds that deflect the light this way or that, or close it off. The blinds were about half open and one of the features of the scope was that it did some kind of digital re-imaging if the view was only partial. This brought me into the room.

There was a lamp on and a couple of people, one standing and one sitting on the sofa. The one standing might have been Mrs. Ryan. She was wearing bikini underwear and I couldn't tell whether she had on a bra or not. I had a booster lens, which I put on and looked again. It was Mrs. Ryan, and she was wearing one of those flesh-toned bras. She had the kind of body that small thin women can keep longer, the body of a teen-ager with an extra fullness. Then I got a glimpse of the guy because he stood up. He was naked and looked disoriented and I had to do a double take. It wasn't the guy from the bar. It looked to me like it was Robbie Robins, who had been in and out of jail and rehab for the last year or so, looking sadder and more pathetic each time *People* covered the story.

I imagined there was some kind of conversa-tion taking place, but there was no direct eye-to-eye exchange. Robbie Robins could have been saying something as he looked in one direction, or Mrs. Ryan saying something looking in another. Two people, one naked and the other almost, standing in a room in East Hollywood. It was getting chillier, and the light wasn't going to last much longer. I would pack up in a little while. I had something to report to Mr. Ryan, although a situation like this is ambiguous and dangerous enough so that I'd have to sort it out after a night's sleep.

When I looked back into the telescope Robins slapped Mrs. Ryan across the face. She went down onto the sofa. A car dealer in Westlake told me that Robins had walked into his Lexus dealership stoned and told him he wanted two of the cars, but when they checked his credit it was denied. How did a millionaire movie star manage that?

26

ANN LANE TOLD ME AT DINNER at Louisa's on Montana that she was moving to the Bay Area. I was disappointed. I'd been holding on to a moment or two with this fresh-faced intelligent young woman as if it might have some more than passing connection with my life, and now it was clear that it didn't. I had more wine than I should have and told her I thought she shouldn't lose her connection with L.A.; I advised her to sublet her apartment rather than give it up. She told me she was already subletting so that wasn't an option.

I walked her back to her apartment complex on Euclid, not far from my place, kissed her chastely on the cheek outside her door and said goodnight.

"Goodnight, Detective Michael," she said. She had had a couple of glasses of Bordeaux herself.

"Detective Shepard—Michael Shepard," I said.

"A good shepherd," she said and went in her front door.

A younger man might have played that moment and found a door into another moment and then another one. I recognized exhaustion when I felt it, though, and turned around and walked the rest of the way home and lay down on my bed.

My machine had a couple of no-show messages, where the computerized voice says, "If you wish to make a call, please hang up and dial again." I knew these were from Stephen calling collect. He was banging up against it now, on a lot of different sides. They had given him Level One Alcohol School, which cost $500, impounded his car, suspended his license, fined him $1,500, and neither his mother nor I was going to pay for any of it. I remembered to thank God for my blessings, not the least of which was that Stephen wasn't seriously hurt or hadn't hurt another person when he had driven away from BJ's drunk.

I got undressed, feeling virtuous for not trying to intrude my life into Ann Lane's where it didn't belong, brushed my teeth, and got into bed. The young film editor who lived in a small apartment directly under the bedroom was practicing his guitar, which gave the room a soft rhythmic thrumming.

I woke up at my usual four in the morning and remembered that I'd forgotten about Samantha, the beauty at Books whom Skeet had spoken to before he poisoned me and made for the hills. It was a serious mistake and it caused me to wonder if I wasn't losing it. I rationalized that I'd been the victim of an attempted murder, and probably had post-traumatic stress disorder.

27

Samantha had jet black hair and very white skin and looked with mostly kind interest on the passing parade of book junkies who frequented Books. But beauty that she was, she had to be careful. I knew she had martial arts training and saw her register a particular customer from time to time with a fine-tuned sense of potential threat. We were in a long running, low-burning argument about the middle generation of novelists Samantha loved and I loved less. When I walked in the store the next morning, she looked up at me from a book at the register and I saw that she was still digesting the sentences. She also might have been nearsighted.

"I come bearing an offer of marriage from Don DeLillo," I said.

"Oh, hi, Michael," she said and gave me her thoughtful smile. "I don't suppose you've read *Falling Man* yet?"

"You suppose right, my dear," I said, perusing the photography books on a shelf beside her. "But enough of this fiddle-faddle . . ." I looked over at her to see what sort of impression I was making. She was looking out the door at the chilly white day but turned back to me. She had a lovely contemplative way about her and I couldn't understand her giving Skeet the time of day.

"Where's Skeet?" I said.

She studied my face and then frowned. "Hey, that's right," she said. "You were here that afternoon."

I'd never told her what I did.

"You read about it in the papers or saw it on the news?"

"I can't believe that of him," Samantha said, looking toward the door abstractedly. "You didn't even say hi that afternoon."

I blew my cover, told her I was a PI, to see what she might tell me.

"There's just one thing I don't get in all this . . ." she said.

"What?"

"How could anyone as spiritual as Skeet be a murderer?"

"Spiritual?" I said. "How do you come up with that word?"

"Well, he is. He's a yogic adept. He's an herbalist. He gave me this mixture that cured my sinuses. He only uses drugs sacramentally . . ."

"Why do I think that means sex?" I said, staring into the middle distance myself now, not to be any more intrusive than I knew I was being. When she didn't say anything I looked back at her.

"I don't think that has anything to do with it."

"Well," I said, temporizing. "Maybe it shouldn't, you know."

I pulled another book from the photography section, trying to let the moment fall away.

"Where was Skeet going that afternoon?"

"Oh," she said, "he wanted to take me up to do the Circle Game, the Human Potential Intensive, in Santa Barbara."

"Really," I said. "I assume you didn't go."

"No, I had to work. I would have liked to—it's so beautiful up there. But Skeet never understands that I have a job."

28

My appointment with Laura Fonseca later that morning was at her home on North Almont Drive in Beverly Hills. I was wondering just how big a star she'd been when I found the address, a small two-story house among a block of two-story houses of the same general look just north of Wilshire. I rang the front doorbell and in a moment she answered. She was still a beauty but her face was a woman's now, whereas in *April Rain* she'd been the perfect dream of adolescence, blond, beautiful, and devoted, with only a shy hint of a mind.

"Mr. Shepard," she said in a good voice that brought back the actress. "Please come in."

She led me into a neat, mostly yellow front room and indicated the white sofa at the center. The cover of *People* magazine that featured Raven and her together when *April Rain* was released was framed among other photographs on a table beside the sofa.

"Can I get you something to drink?"

"Thanks, I'm fine," I said sitting down.

"Well, then," she said, taking a seat on the other side of the glass-topped coffee table in front of the sofa, "shall I just begin?"

"That would be great."

"Well, as you know, I knew Val Raven and, through Val, I had some contact with Skeet. I was an inexperienced girl, fresh from acting school in Minneapolis when I got the role in *April Rain*. I'd had a crush on Val Raven in high school, ever since I saw *Hollywood High*. So—"

She sighed. "I was in heaven when he took me under his wing. It was what you'd call a rude awakening, complicated by my falling head over heels in love."

She stopped for a moment.

"I was a young girl in love . . ."

She looked away again.

"They were lovers," she said and looked back at me again, "which I couldn't see at the time, and only dawned on me after Val disappeared. There were a million little telltale signs, and they even wanted me in a threesome, I see now, both of them dropping broad hints. Skeet answering the door naked one time when I went over to meet Val. Well, in this business, the kind of men who do this, you have to be so self-involved—it's what protects you from the fact that you're just a lowly actor, a pawn in the game plan of a big machine that will replace you soon enough unless you happen to ensconce yourself. And that has its drawbacks, too. Look at all the great actors, just incredible talents, who have had these huge, but actually rather silly careers. Well, I'm off on a tangent."

"What do you do now?" I said.

"I got my masters in clinical psychology at UCLA. I have a small practice."

"Congratulations."

29

LATER THAT AFTERNOON I WAS AT the office working on a report for Jake Ryan. I didn't identify Robbie Robins and hadn't photographed the scene, which I might have done with the scope I'd rented. I could have taken Stephen or, say, Laura Fonseca to London on the proceeds from *The Enquirer* or *The Star.* The word was Robins was speedballing, injecting

combinations of heroin and cocaine, a procedure that regularly proved fatal. The question
was whether Mrs. Ryan was also doing that, and
if she was, whether some decisive rehab action
could be taken.

In the middle of the report, Amy told me Laura
Fonseca was calling.

I picked up the phone.

"I've decided I want to hire you. I want you to
find him. He needs to be put away. Val and now
this girl. In some way I guess I feel implicated."

I asked how she'd heard about me.

"Detective Axelson speaks very highly of you."

When I put down the phone I looked across
the room.

"Oh, she's got a new fan now," Amy said.

I GOT THE LISTING FOR THE Circle Game, which
turned out to be in Montecito, just south of and
even ritzier than Santa Barbara. I called the
number and said I was interested in signing up
for the intensive. I was transferred to a man
named John Summer, who came on the line as if
he already knew me.

"Michael?" he said.

"Yes."

"How're you doing?" I could hear that he was smiling.

"Pretty well," I said.

He told me that they happened to have a space for that week's intensive and asked whether that would work with my schedule. I said that I was ready to do it, so the sooner the better.

"Okay," he said. "I hear that you're ready and that's just great, so let me get a couple of things down over the phone since we don't have time to mail out the application. I'm also going to need a credit card number."

We got these details out of the way and then he said he wanted to know three things that I wanted to get out of the Circle Game in order of their importance to me.

I told him I wanted to improve my relationship with my son.

"Great," he said. "And the other two?"

"Well," I said, but couldn't think of what came next.

"Alright," he said, "think about it for a while and call me back here." He gave me another number.

"Now," he said. "Here's the thing to realize. You're due up here on Thursday morning at 8 a.m., but as of right now you're in the Game. Okay?"

"You mean it's started now?"

"That's right. It's going on as we speak."

"Yes?" Amy said when I put down the phone.

"I'm in the Circle Game right now," I said.

30

"MICHAEL," JOHN SUMMER SAID, "I DON'T know what to make of this. Can you help me out here?"

It was after midnight and I had snuck into an office at the Circle Game after we'd been dismissed for the night.

"John," I said, sitting on the floor with the file drawer open between my legs, "I think I can be straight with you about this, although it embarrasses me to be in this situation."

When he'd taken my application over the phone, I'd puzzled a moment after he'd asked me what I did and then told him I was a writer/producer. He'd asked me at dinner what I was working on and I'd said a true crime movie, information he took in with a kind of proprietary pride, I thought.

"Until I've heard something," he said, "I've got a pretty harsh procedure facing us both now. I call security and all hell breaks loose. My advice to you is to get real—fast."

"Thank you," I said, having learned that day that in accepting a bad situation one begins to overcome it. "Look, John," I said, "you know the business I'm in is highly competitive, and sometimes the truth can get shoved aside in the interests of the almighty dollar, but I've been trying to follow this thing out so that it doesn't turn into just another sixties-bashing bonanza. You know, Manson's getting married but most of the good guys are off the planet and we've just about bottomed out, and I just want to make sure there isn't something I'm missing here." I paused for a breath.

"I don't know what you're talking about," he said from the doorway.

"I'm surprised you haven't heard from some of my other colleagues about this," I said. "I mean people in the business. Although frankly it doesn't surprise me," I said, "because with all the elements in place, why do more homework?"

He was shaking his head from side to side, as if he regretted what he was obliged to do. I knew it would involve being arrested, hauled off to some half-empty local processing tank and an emergency call to Axelson that would blow my cover. "Look, John," I said. "A performance artist-poet named Skeet is wanted in connection with two murders, including the murder of Val Raven. I'm sure you know that."

His face changed.

"Well, *Jesus*," John Summer said. "Why didn't you say so? I almost brought that up to *you* at dinner. I would have, if the others hadn't been there, because we can't have this kind of thing circulating at our seminars.

"Look," he said, "we both know there's an HBO miniseries here. I saw that immediately. But I . . ." He sighed. "I just don't have the connections.

"But this isn't the way to go about these things," he said. "You've broken laws."

31

I DROVE HOME THAT NIGHT. THERE were two copies of the *Times* on my steps. I gathered them up, went in my front door, and laid them down on the pine table by the big window opposite the kitchenette. A sliver of a face caught my eye on one of the front pages. I put down my keys, took off most of my clothes, and then before getting into the shower, walked back to the table and opened the paper. It was another one of those ghastly headshots of Robbie Robins, looking sleepless and disheveled. The story said an emergency call had brought police and an ambulance crew to the Gaylord, where they'd discovered Robins alone, naked, and unconscious in an apartment owned by someone unnamed who was out of town. Robins was still unconscious in Intensive Care at Cedar Sinai Hospital. Police were looking for a woman who had been seen at the Bounty with him over the past week.

It was nine thirty so I called Amy at the office, but she hadn't arrived yet. I texted her and she rang back.

"Jake Ryan has to talk to you."

"Thanks. I'll call him right away."

"How'd it go?"

"Okay. I'll tell you about it."

I called Ryan, who sounded shaken. He told me that Mrs. Ryan was asleep in the Brentwood house. He said she had a drug problem, he was certain of it, and wanted to know what I could do. I waited for him to say something about Robins but he didn't. I asked whether there was any chance Mrs. Ryan might wake up and go somewhere.

"She sleeps pretty heavily," he said. "We were up late. I saw some . . . well . . ." He stopped. I figured he'd seen some tracks on her.

I gave him my cell number and asked him to let me know if he thought she was going to go anywhere. In the meantime, I would look into the possibility of an intervention.

"That's what it comes to, I guess. She's an addict. I thought addicts weren't interested in sex."

"Are you sure that sex is a part of what's going on?"

"I can tell you there's less of it with me."

I CALLED A FRIEND NAMED BRIAN Heraldson and told him I needed him for an intervention.

"Jesus Christ, I just woke up. How are you?" He laughed. "It's been a long time. What have you got?"

"Yeah, it has." We had worked on getting the daughter of a television star into Van Nuys Psychiatric Facility in 2000, and I recognized then how good he was with addicts. "It's a little complicated," I said.

"It always is, sweetie." He laughed again, crashing off into a fit of coughing. He was a recovering heroin addict, in recovery for close to two decades, during which time he'd found a new vocation helping other addicts. Before that, he'd been a Jesuit priest.

It would have to be in mid-afternoon, Brian said, and we needed to talk first. It was a relief to hear that: I needed sleep. I invited him to my apartment at three that day and then called Jake Ryan and told him we'd be at the Brentwood house at four. Then I got in the shower. When I got out, I set the bedroom alarm for two thirty and drew the blinds and lay down and listened to the kids in the Lincoln Middle School at their Friday recess. I had gone to the Hawthorne School in Beverly Hills one year of my childhood and I remembered a girl named Betty there, a blond who was lithe and pretty and made my blood run faster when I was nine.

32

BRIAN ARRIVED ON TIME, GRINNING, PERUSING
the apartment, one of those men who would look
virtually the same from their mid-forties to their
mid-sixties: thinning blond-gray hair, some tight-
ening about the neck, and a bland banker's face.

"Well, what the hell happened to you?" he said,
standing up from a quick run-through of a corner
bookcase in the living room.

"It happens," I said. "Why would a sane woman want to be married to an only middling PI after the age of forty-five? I've got some fresh-brewed Starbucks. Sit down over by the window there."

"That's fine. I want to check your reading. *Middlemarch*?" He thumbed the paperback I had at the top of the pile by the wood chest.

"What are you reading?" I said.

"Oscar Wilde. The plays. Like fresh-cut flowers with the morning dew still on them."

"I'll check it out," I said.

I poured him a cup of coffee and one for myself and brought both out to the table in front of the window. He sat down, smiling, and I told him about the case.

"She's an actress?" he said. "See, we addicts have these exaggerated nervous systems. It's some kind of genetic fumble: we like a kind of excitement that isn't out there anymore except on the end of a needle. Or maybe it puts that hunger to rest. You know, in the old days you had to watch out for tomahawks and wandering bears and whatnot, and hew out a place in the wilderness. Nowadays, you're given an iPad at birth to keep you properly pacified. Pretty soon they'll have 'em out in space, little capsules orbiting the universe—an iPad and a man, or an iPad and a woman, in a death embrace, cosmic trash. And we thought TV was bad!"

He locked onto the middle distance, staring into my house.

"Alright," he said. "We can use the Robbie Robins thing as leverage. We're going to need every bit of leverage we've got. Why should she go to Betty Ford? She has a previous engagement. But if prison was the only other option she might be more open to it."

33

I THOUGHT I SHOULD PROBABLY BRING Jake Ryan up to speed on his wife's connection with Robbie Robins, but first I'd see where Mrs. Ryan was and how difficult things were going to be. Brian followed me in his cream Lincoln Town Car and parked behind me in front of the Ryans' two-story house on Clearwood, a quiet Brentwood street south of Sunset. I went up the brick walkway to the front door and rang the doorbell, one of those chimes you could hear from outside. Ryan answered the door in dark slacks and a red T-shirt and was barefoot. He was unshaven and looked tired.

"Yeah, come on in," he said. "This is tough." He led me into a big modern kitchen with a white-tiled centerpiece with barstools beside it. Mrs. Ryan, sat on a stool in a big navy blue robe. She had black coffee in a white porcelain cup.

"Who's this?" she said to her husband when I'd followed him into the room.

"Lori, this is Michael Shepard, a friend I thought might be able to help us."

"Fuck." She rolled her eyes.

I looked over at Ryan and he was looking away from his wife, staring into a corner of the kitchen.

"Mrs. Ryan," I said, "I'm a private investigator. As you probably know, a woman who fits your description was seen in and around the Gaylord with Robbie Robins."

Ryan looked at me.

"Who the fuck is *this*?" Mrs. Ryan yelled at her husband. "What did you do?"

"Nothing," he said. "I didn't do a fucking thing, okay?"

But she was already off the stool and gone from the kitchen and Ryan followed her. I walked out of the kitchen and then out of the house through the front door. I walked down to Brian in the driver's seat of the Lincoln.

"Did she just scream?" he said.

"I screwed up," I said standing beside his car.

"No, you didn't. The cat's out of the bag. This may take time now. If she runs, they can pick her up on a felony arrest warrant."

"What's the felony?"

"Well, heroin, and she maybe gave him the hot shot, right?"

"I haven't got a clue . . ."

"Give this guy some space." He started his car. "Text me if you need me."

I watched him pull out and drive down the street.

34

JAKE RYAN HAD MY CELL NUMBER, but I didn't expect him to call. It was an impossible situation. If Robbie Robins died, then maybe they'd issue a felony warrant if someone had identified Mrs. Ryan at the Gaylord. But otherwise there really wasn't a lot that could be done. Her vocal instrument was strong and healthy and until she got further down the line, what was to stop her?

When I got home, I put the cups and saucers from Brian's visit in the sink and did a little housework. Then I sat down on the sofa and picked up *Middlemarch* and read the scene between Dorothea and Ladislaw where neither confesses their love for each other and Ladislaw abruptly takes his leave for a new life somewhere.

I wanted to give Laura Fonseca a report on Skeet, but didn't really have anything worth reporting. I was restless, though, and knew I wouldn't be able to sleep now. She picked up the phone on the first ring.

"It's Michael Shepard, I . . ."

"Yes, Mr. Shepard . . ."

"I went up to Santa Barbara for a day and started to do the Circle Game. It was the last place we know Skeet headed."

"I did the Circle Game. . . . What did you think of it? Well, I know. Why don't you join me for dinner?"

"I will if I'm buying. I don't want to put you out."

"Nonsense. I'm already cooking. I guess I've assumed you don't have a wife. Am I way off?"

35

I BROUGHT OVER A BOTTLE OF Bordeaux that
went back and forth between us over the course
of fillet of sole, boiled potatoes, and a green
salad with sliced-up slivers of almonds. We
lingered over the dessert of split pears with a
little honey and espressos, and ended up talking
about my son.

"Does he have ADHD?" she said.

"We think so, but he's never been tested. I read a book and he seemed to match up pretty much across the board. Then I passed the book on to him, and he read a couple of pages and said it sounded like him."

"It's probably hard for him to read."

"He needs the military, or some other tightly controlled environment, which I don't want to be prison. He responds beautifully to discipline, and I was, and my wife was, a product of the sixties, so . . ."

"That wasn't your thing."

"A couple of times, when I needed to settle him down at night when he was eight or nine, I spanked him. I've always wondered about that. The odd thing was it settled him right down."

It had been some time since I'd sat down to a dinner in a home with candles on the table. Laura Fonseca clearly knew and liked domestic arts, and I appreciated that less casually these days.

I started to help her take the dishes from the table to the sink, but she told me to leave them. I followed her out to the living room. We were at the living room sofa when she turned around and looked up at me, and in the play of the moment I ended up holding her in my arms.

"So many problems," she said, looking up at me and holding my shoulder. "I have to watch my tendency to be codependent."

We sat down together on the sofa. There was classical piano music playing softly. The lights were on but not brightly and then we were kissing.

36

J<small>AKE</small> R<small>YAN</small> <small>WANTED TO SUE ME</small> because what I'd started to say to Mrs. Ryan made her run away. A day or two later Robbie Robins recovered and was released from the hospital. Brian talked to Mr. Ryan after I talked to him, but he remained angry.

I didn't hear from Stephen and wondered what was going on with him and prayed for him to live

God's will for his life. I prayed the same thing for myself, and for Vera, and for Laura Fonseca. I told her I'd give her her money back and she said to keep it and use it when there was a break in the case.

Axelson dropped me and/or the case for more pressing matters. I had to cut Amy's hours, and she started singing on Wednesday nights at Largo. Laura and I went one night and apparently there was something about the movie star and the detective in one of the Hollywood columns. Winter and spring came and went with a small number of clients and my regular work with Efren De Guzman in Torrance. One July night, after I'd driven home in a red summer sky from another meeting of the Torrance Private Industry Council, I came into the apartment as my cell was ringing.

"Michael?"

"Yes?"

"It's Ann Lane."

"Ann, how are you?"

"I'm up in Fairfax. In Marin County, you know the Bay Area, and I'm a little scared," she said.

"I used to live there," I said pointlessly.

She was performing in a coffee house in San Rafael, and the other night this guy with red hair and black eyebrows had come over to her and started to talk and she'd realized it was Skeet.

"Did he try to hide it?" I asked.

"No. That was what was so crazy. He didn't say anything one way or another. And didn't say he knew me, but I was sure it was him."

"Did he change his voice?"

"Slightly maybe, but . . ."

"What?" I said.

"It was almost like he *was* someone else."

"Meaning what—he got a designer brain?"

"Yeah, or a lobotomy. Or he had some kind of Tony Robbins neuro-linguistic reprogramming done, you know? So he's Joe Rock. That's his name now. It's really so creepy."

"It sounds like he's crazy. Do you know where he lives?"

"Are you kidding? I'm scared I'm going to see him again."

She told me her number, and I blocked out the schedule she was on for the next two weeks. She had a show coming up in Seattle in ten days. She thought Skeet might try to reach her again.

"If he does, see if you can find out where he lives. I'm going to try to get up there. In the meantime, you may be hearing from the police."

37

I WAS SITTING ON MY BED when the call ended. It was summertime again. My neighbor's small son was laughing riotously. His mother, a single mom who worked in real estate, was laughing too. But the chill was there now, the way it hadn't been for a while. I didn't like the idea of this madman in the vicinity of Ann Lane's delicacy, clarity, and slight flakiness.

"He's got another name?" Axelson said on the phone. "He could be in a fugue state, like an amnesia that sometimes happens in these cases. We know he's a serial, and that state is known to trigger violence. I'll call a police guy I know in SF. Who's the woman?"

I told him about Ann Lane.

"I don't know whether they'll let me go for this, but it's going to be a day or two even if they do. What about you?"

"The sooner the better. I guess I'll just drive up there."

"I need all the details before you leave."

It was day's worth of driving I hadn't done in years. I got out some CDs and threw some stuff in the car. Laura had a friend in Mill Valley and arranged for me to stay with her.

AT SOME POINT DRIVING ALONG THE Pacific Coast Highway in Ventura County at around ten thirty the next morning (I waited till rush hour ended before I took off), it occurred to me that, one, I was too old for this, and two, I was scared and angry about this head case in our midst.

I didn't get to Mill Valley because a lieutenant with the Marin County PD called and asked me to drive to a house in Fairfax.

"What's wrong?" I said.

"It's not good, I'm sorry. She'd been living in the upstairs apartment there for the last month."

"Ann Lane."

"I'm sorry. It must have happened right after we contacted her. We want you to see this before they take the body."

38

"I'VE BEEN TALKING TO SHRINKS ALL day," Axelson told me that evening on the phone. "The guy isn't stupid but I assume we've got a leg up if he doesn't know who the fuck he is."

"I'm going to the Bard in San Rafael tonight, the place where she was performing."

"He may have run. If not, we've got an

advantage here," he said again. I could hear how badly he wanted him.

I watched a play with a lot of words at the Bard that night, and tried to find Skeet/ Joe Rock among many painted hairdos, males with earrings, and women with alert looks and hard laughter. It wasn't my old Marin crowd by many miles.

There was a kid at the bar with a leather jacket and half his head of hair shaved away. The other side was blond and spiked. I looked at him and toasted him with my house ale.

His name was Martin Barnes. It could take him a while, he told me, to find Joe Rock, who was, he said, a dealer. If the product was good, I said, it could be the first of a series of buys, gave him the cell number and left.

39

THE SAN FRANCISCO CHRONICLE LAY ON the breakfast table in the light-filled, cheerful kitchen. Janet Gabriel, a transplanted Angeleno who looked to be in her late forties or early fifties, had a decorating business with a small shop in San Anselmo. She was about to leave for work.

"I'm an early riser," she said. When you get to be our age, you must work or go mad. Don't you agree?"

"I do," I said.

"Well, that's why Laura adores you. You're a *mensch*. Now, I'd make you a proper breakfast but I've got an early appointment," she said and gave me a quick international-style "buss" on one side of my face and then the other.

When she left I poured myself a cup of coffee and sat down with the *Chronicle*. No more Herb Caen. The wife of a newly elected congressman who was caught up in a sexting scandal said her estranged husband worked inhuman hours and needed a twelve-step program for Internet porn, which had become his home away from home.

"These people are worked too hard to have normal lives," the lady told reporters in a press conference that was given front page coverage. The cell rang.

"Martin Barnes here. Is that Mike?"

"Thanks for getting back to me."

"Yes, well. I ran into Joe Rock last night and he'll be at this outdoor café, Zeema's, near the library in San Anselmo this afternoon around two thirty? Do you know where that is?"

"I'll find it. So you're the broker?" I said.

"I can't really say. He asked me to be there. He's checking you out, I guess."

"That's fine. Around two thirty then."

"See you then. Oh! Bring four hundred dollars in twenties and fifties. No checks or money orders."

40

I met Axelson at the Fourth Street Café in San Rafael at eleven thirty, the scene of a long-ago breakfast or two when I was breaking in with the Marin P. D. He'd taken an early flight to Oakland that morning and was in touch with the Marin police. A detective had been assigned to us and would be meeting us at the San Anselmo Library, Axelson said, before the stakeout at Zeema's. The lieutenant looked tired.

"I gather this maniac may be burning his bridges, so we'll need to watch ourselves."

We sat at the counter. He had an untouched cup of coffee in front of him. Ann Lane's death had rattled us both.

ZEEMA'S WAS JUST OFF THE MAIN street with its little shops and restaurants. The afternoon crowd had filled most of the outside tables. It was an intermittently sunny afternoon. Axelson was at another table not too close by. The detective, Robbie Collins, who looked like a surfer, was parked across the street in an unmarked white Prius.

"I DON'T SEE THE ROCK MAN," Martin Barnes said finding my table and taking a seat. He'd turned a few heads in the crowd as he came along. San Anselmo wasn't new wave, if that was what he was.

"Have you got the cash?" he said sotto voce.

I indicated the inside breast pocket of my leather jacket.

"I need to see it." I put the envelope down on the table. The sun had come out again onto the table.

A dowager type was making her way out.

"Oh," Barnes said. He stood up, and the lady took the envelope.

I stood up.

"No, dearie," she said, "please don't get up."

I felt an electric jolt in my side and staggered back against the table.

41

I WENT BACK TO JANET GABRIEL'S guest room in the Mill Valley place and lay down on the bed in my clothes, thinking I'd take them off in a moment but dozed off, my brain still hurling around corners in the back of the Prius with Collins at the wheel chasing Skeet in a yellow VW bug all over to hell and gone and losing him in the warehouse area of San Rafael.

Several hours later, when I'd opened my eyes again in the dark room and was lying awake without having moved, the cell went off.

"I can't sleep," Axelson said. "Meet me at the bar down here, unless you're asleep."

"He was a quick jog up the freeway at the hotel beside the movie theater in San Rafael.

I found him in a booth at the hotel bar. I sat down and then went for the back end of the dark bench so that I could raise my left leg onto the seat. My ankle was bothering me. A waitress came by and I ordered an Amstel Light.

"If you're not a star at a certain age, and you want the world's attention, maybe you decide to go out this way. Remember the Unabomber," he said.

"You ever read the manifesto?"

"Kill for peace," he said. "Exactly. The wires can get tangled after forty. Sanity is this precious commodity.

"That detective is something behind the wheel," he added.

42

I was back at Janet Gabriel's at around one that night and got undressed in the guest room. I got into bed and thumbed through a paperback novel on the bed table: Sultry women with stunted relationships with the most important men in the world. Children shunted off with sultry governesses who didn't mind something on the side with the important guy. Then the governess started thinking straight about some stuff that confused the guy, helping him in his role as a ruler of the new world order. It seemed to me that I could sell my business. I wasn't thinking clearly or was already asleep.

There was some sort of fluttering in the room a little before dawn and then Laura was in bed with me, huddled up against my back.

"Hi," she said. "I missed you."

A couple of hours later, I got up and tried not to wake her as I got dressed.

43

WHILE I WAS IN THE KITCHEN making coffee, Axelson phoned.

"We've got a new lead. Some of the bills turned up."

"Bills?"

"The bills for the drug buy were marked—and they got deposited last night in the grocery store ATM in Bolinas."

"Bolinas. . . . Logical, I guess. "

"How so?"

"It's sort of the outlaw town in Marin, except these days it takes a couple of mill for a modest house. It's where they found Brautigan."

"Clayton says it's about an hour. Can you be ready in ten minutes?"

HILARY SHANE, AN OLDER WOMAN WITH close-cropped salt-and-pepper hair and a gentle face, was in the back seat of the Prius, and I got in beside her. She was a psychiatric doctor who specialized in Skeet-type cases.

"All of this may go back to being undefended in some moment of childhood abuse," she said, "so that the psyche needed another personality to handle the problem."

"This is the multiple angle," Axelson said without turning around. "Frankly it's a little hard to follow."

I leaned back against my seat and looked through my window up at the sky, blue with a few clouds. In a little while we got into the rural plains around Olema before taking a left onto Route 1 to Bolinas. The rolling hills of West

Marin—so beautiful it made me wonder why I ever left. It was around eleven in the morning when we got into town.

44

WE HAD ROOMS IN THE HOTEL that abutted
Smiley's, the downtown bar. Each of us in a
second-floor room with a shower. I'd spent a
couple of evenings in Smiley's before I entered
the Police Academy and looked out the window
across the street at Scowley's, a cave-like restaurant
run by the Fontaine brothers, a couple of witty
roughnecks.

In the dark restaurant, Dr. Shane and I decided to be a tourist couple and Collins and Axelson would snoop around separately.

"He may be holed up somewhere," Robbie said. "I'll check the guest houses."

"Why don't you and Dr. Shane take a walk, then," Axelson said to me. "Oh, and here."

He gave me a miniature walkie-talkie.

"Push this," he said, showing me a button marked A, "and I'm on the line." There was another button marked B.

Outside was the raw underlying roar of most coastal places. West Marin wasn't as mild as the inland towns.

We walked down the road to the beach and stopped while Dr. Shane pulled some sandals out of her purse to negotiate the sand, tucking her brown flats into her bag. It wasn't a very long walk to the road at the other end of the downtown. A few parents and kids were scattered here and there with towels on the sand. There was a three-story modern beach house with big windows as we left the sand for the street. It had once been the scene of a drug bust involving rock stars that made the Marin papers. This was the town that kept the sixties going when it had expired nearly everywhere else. Maybe he had customers here?

We walked past a teashop and then waited at the light to cross Brighton Road. On the other side was a little hotel, the Coastal Arms. We walked up the steps to the entrance and went inside and sat down in the lobby. I was on a leather sofa and Dr. Shane on a nearby leather chair.

The lobby had that chiaroscuro light, dark with the brightness of the seaside light outside. People came and went.

I pressed the A button and told Axelson where we were.

45

"I'D LIKE TO BE AROUND HERE now for the last hour or so of light," Axelson said.

Nothing turned up and after a day's worth of wandering around, we were gathering at an outside table at Gwen's sandwich shop, catty corner between our hotel and the grocery store. Then Robbie came out of the entrance of the grocery store and walked over to our table.

"There's a guy in line with a tweed jacket with elbow patches," he said. "That couldn't be him, could it?"

"Can you see the ring finger of his right hand?" Dr. Shane asked. "He's got a little peace sign tattoo on it."

"Really?" I said.

"It's in his police file . . ."

"I'll be back," Robbie said.

46

FOR THE NEXT COUPLE OF HOURS we kept him in
our sights. The big house that fronted on the
beach that Dr. Shane and I had passed that
morning had been remodeled as a B&B, and
Skeet—the tattoo was the positive ID—was
staying in a room on the third floor. I knocked
on the door a little before ten that night. Axelson
was down the hall; Collins was closer to me on

the wall beside the door. We were going to arrest him. A minute later with Axelson, Collins, and me all in the room, and Skeet under arrest sitting in an upholstered chair, he recognized me.

"Redding, right?" he said.

Then with one hand he shot lighter fluid onto me, and then an extended flame shot from his other hand and ignited me.

Every atom of energy in me focused and I leaped on him. Some thoughts came to me:

1. I'm on fire.
2. He set me on fire.
3. I think I'm on fire, but maybe I'm not.
4. He shot me with lighter fluid.
5. He's a fucking moron.
6. I'm going to kill him.
7. I'm strong.
8. He isn't so strong.

I let him roll over me, and even allowed that he might hold me down, but had no doubt about the outcome.

Then some kinetic change happened and I was barely making it. He was stronger than I was. My breath went short and harsh. I was on my left side,

Skeet was pushing me down so that I'd go onto my stomach. I thought:

1. Where's my backup?
2. Somebody knock him out.
3. Or kill him.
4. I'm extremely tired.
5. I'm about to give up.
6. Where am I?
7. Why didn't I shoot him?
8. Laura . . . Laura Fonseca.

My right hand touched something and there was a quickened response. It was his nose. I stuck the third finger of my right hand into his nostril.

He made a noise and my chest filled up with oxygen again.

"It's okay, Michael," Robbie said. "We got him."

I could smell him, a weird honey-tinged shit odor. It the smell of fear, I think.

"It's alright, Mike," Axelson said. "It's okay, we've got him."

Eventually my hand unclenched and I let go and rolled away from him.

"We've got an ambulance coming, Mike," Axelson said.

47

IT WAS A WEEK AFTER I'D returned to Santa
Monica, and three days after my surgery, that
Skeet was brought back and held without bail at
the Los Angeles County Jail pending his preliminary hearing date. Dr. Shane was lobbying with
signatures from various psychiatric eminences to
have him put into a mental institution rather
than the Chino Institute for Men.

We had coffee one afternoon at the Coffee Bean on Montana, sitting at an outside table in the mild afternoon. I had a new bandage now and was told the cosmetic surgery had gone smoothly. I was trying to understand her. In time Skeet could perhaps coalesce as a normal single identity, she believed.

Sometimes at night I woke up and knew I wouldn't sleep anymore.

"He could actually do us some good," Dr. Shane said, "if we can learn about how this mechanism works."

"In other words, he's a scientific experiment. Isn't that dehumanizing, too?"

"Not as much as being executed, or for that matter, warehoused for the rest of his life."

HE WAS BROUGHT HANDCUFFED TO THE defense table at the preliminary hearing. He sat at the table, from time to time looking dully around. He was on Thorazine or some other anti-psychotic.

The prosecuting attorney, a handsome straight-arrow named Dan Pisonetti, took the position that Skeet was malingering with the multiple person-ality scenario, that he had simply duped Dr. Shane.

"Your honor," he said, "criminals have been known to dress up in various disguises when they commit crimes. That doesn't make them clinically insane."

The public defender was a decent man named Orville Smith who had his work cut out for him. Short, prematurely balding and soft-featured, he lacked Pisonetti's charisma. While Dr. Shane could provide him with a broad-stroked sketch of his client's mind, it was another thing to sell that to a jury. Smith was able to get a delay of a month while he studied the case further. He and Axelson and Dr. Shane and I had coffee after the hearing in the courthouse cafeteria.

"This guy reminds me of a new Android app," Smith said quietly.

48

VERA TOLD ME STEPHEN HAD BEEN sleeping in a
friend's van.

I drove out to a gas station at the corner of
Rancho Conejo and Hillcrest Drive right off the
101, where Stephen asked me to meet him. He was
sitting on the cement curb of a flowerbed planting
when I drove in. He stood up immediately and
looked alright, a little heavier than I'd last seen him.

"What happened to your face?" he said.

"Nothing," I said. "Why?"

He chuckled. "Oh my God, you got some kind of a face lift. Or is it Botox?"

He ordered a beer at lunch at the Oaktree West restaurant in the North Ranch Mall across the shopping plaza from BJ's, where he'd lost it that night. He had a job doing data entry for a computer firm in Westlake Village, having lost his security officer job after his arrest. A coworker gave him a ride to work and back since his license was suspended.

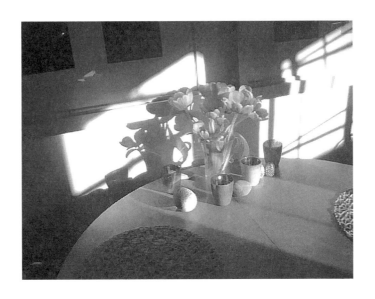

49

Skeet tried to hang himself the day before his trial was to begin in downtown Los Angeles Superior Court. They upped his anti-psychotic medicine. Jury selection took two weeks, and the trial phase was briefer than anyone expected, three and a half weeks. Pisonetti had agreed to settle for a sentence of life in prison without parole and not to seek the death penalty.

Smith went for Not Guilty by Reason of Insanity, and Dr. Shane, who now had a grant to work with the accused, was his star witness and detailed the mechanism of multiple personality disorder and the proper clinical treatment. Pisonetti's closing statement, which I read about in the *L.A. Times*, featured big blow-ups of photographs of the three known victims—Val Raven, Anita Holbrook, and Ann Lane—and the implication that there may have been others, albeit the judge had sustained Smith's objection.

After closing statements and instructions by the judge, the jury took a day and a half to come back with a guilty of First Degree Murder verdict. I took the afternoon off to go to the sentencing with Laura. Ann Lane's mother, who had come from the East Coast for the sentencing, sat beside me. When the judge pronounced life without the possibility of parole, she was weeping. I held her for a moment. Laura sat on the other side of her.

As we were leaving a tall man about my age approached me just outside the courthouse door.

"Mr. Shepard?" he said.

"Yes," I said, letting Laura move past me with Mrs. Lane.

"I'm Ron Holbrook, Anita's father. I want to thank you."

I looked into his face and could see a lot of his daughter. We shook hands.

"I'm very sorry about your daughter," I said. "She was a fine young woman."

"Thank you," he said.

We were both having a hard time.

I shook his hand again.

Laura was waiting for me in the lobby.

"Mrs. Lane's gone back to Virginia," she said. "My car's downstairs."

She drove me home on the 10 West.

We took a walk while it was still light and then had dinner at the Montana Cafe. After dinner, we walked back to my place in the night.

It was starting to get cool again. I woke up in the middle of the night and realized I needed to shut the windows.

"What're you doing?" Laura said when I got back into bed.

"Closing the windows. It's cold suddenly."

"Please don't turn on the heat, honey," she said. "It ruins my skin."

"Okay," I said. When I couldn't go back to sleep, I went out into the living room to find something to read.

I switched the light on by the chair and ottoman, and then went back and closed the bedroom door so the light wouldn't disturb her. She slept better than I did, but that was an old story. The truth is, over the years I've come to love this hour or so of reading in the dead of night.

ABOUT THE AUTHOR

ARAM SAROYAN IS THE AUTHOR OF the true crime Literary Guild selection *Rancho Mirage*, as well as many other books of prose and poetry. His *Complete Minimal Poems* received the 2008 William Carlos Williams Award from the Poetry Society of America. He is featured in the documentary film *One Quick Move or I'm Gone: Jack Kerouac at Big Sur* and his comments appear in the oral biographies *George Being George: George Plimpton's Life* and *Salinger*.